Aches

written by John Lockyer
illustrated by Kelvin Hawley

Lots of unhappy animals went to visit wise Dr. Owl.
Some had bad pains and others had nasty aches.
They were all moaning and groaning because they felt
sick and sore. They wanted clever Dr. Owl to fix their
sore places and make them feel well again.

3

First, Mouse climbed up the trunk of Dr. Owl's tree.
"What is wrong with you?" asked the doctor.
"My voice sounds squeaky whenever I try to talk,"
squeaked Mouse.

4

After Dr. Owl looked inside Mouse's mouth, he gave her a small bottle of yellow oil.

"Take two teaspoons of oil twice a day," he hooted. "That should get rid of your squeaks."

"Thank you, Doctor," said Mouse. "I feel quite a bit better already."

Next, Snake slithered up the tree trunk.
"Whenever the snake charmer plays music on his
flute," hissed Snake, "I get tangled in knots. I still
have one in my tail."
Dr. Owl looked at the tight, tangled knot.
"What music does the snake charmer play?" he asked.
"Do, ti, la, so, fa, mi, re, do," Snake hissed.

"That's not right!" hooted Dr. Owl. "I think you get tangled in knots because the snake charmer is playing the music backwards. Listen! It should sound like this." Dr. Owl began to play, "Do, re, mi, fa, so, la, ti, do." As Snake twisted and curled in the air, the knot in his tail slowly untangled.

"Thank you," he hissed. "I feel a lot better already."

Kangaroo walked slowly along under Dr. Owl's tree.
"I've lost my hop," she called. "My bounce has gone."
Dr. Owl flew down to check Kangaroo's legs.
"You're right," he said. "Your legs have no hop or
bounce or skip."

He gave Kangaroo a large jar. "Take one of these three times a day," he said "They will soon put the bounce back into your step." Kangaroo looked into the jar. "These are just beans," she said in a surprised voice. "Yes," said Dr. Owl. "But they aren't ordinary beans. They are jumping beans."
"Thanks, Doctor," said Kangaroo. "I feel better already."

When Laughing Hyena came to talk to Dr. Owl, his ears
and his tail hung down. "Nothing seems funny any more,"
he said sadly. "I can't laugh at anything."
Dr. Owl looked into Hyena's ears and eyes.
"I can't find anything wrong," he said.
Hyena said, "You have made everyone else feel well.
You must help me, please."

10

"The other animals were easy to fix," said Dr. Owl.
"What would you give a mouse with a squeaky voice?"
"I don't know," said Hyena, shaking his head.
"She needs two teaspoons of oil twice a day,"
hooted Dr. Owl. That made Hyena smile.

"How do you get a snake charmer's snake to twist
himself into knots?" asked Dr. Owl.
Hyena shook his head again.
"Just play the snake charming music backwards,"
hooted Dr. Owl.
Hyena grinned when he heard that.

12

"What do you give a kangaroo who has lost her hop
and bounce?" asked Dr. Owl.
"I don't know what would fix that," said Hyena.
"Jumping beans three times a day," hooted Dr. Owl.
Hyena laughed loudly. "Ha, ha, ha! Thanks, Doctor.
I feel better already. Ha, ha, ha!"

13

At last, after all the animals had left, Dr. Owl flew
back into his tree house. "What a busy day," he
moaned and groaned to Mrs. Owl. "Fixing animals is
hard work. I feel so tired and sore. I have a pain in
my back, and my head aches."

Mrs. Owl smiled. "Sit down and rest," she said. "I'll bring you a nice hot cup of green leaf tea to fix your aches and pains."

Dr. Owl hopped onto a big soft pile of leaves in the corner. "Thank you," he said. "I'm starting to feel much better already."